Clyde the Cable Car rode on a track
to the background sound of clickety-clack.
But his passengers got their biggest bang
when Clyde rang out with his magical Clang.

4

One day in May, Clyde went for a ride to sound off his Clang which filled him with pride. While his cable car brothers went "ring-a-ding-ding,"

Clyde tried to go Clang,
but could only go Cling.

He cried, "My goodness"
and "Oh, ding-dang it"
I don't want to Cling it,
I just want to Clang it.

He looked around all over the town
and asked the lady at Lost and Found.

"Listen," she said, "and wherever you go, you can hear the sounds of San Francisco.

'I left my heart' some singer sang.
If he found his heart you can find your Clang."

So he rode on out to Fisherman's Wharf where
Sasha the Sea Lion went "Orf, Orf, Orf."
"That's fine," Said Clyde, "for your sea lion gang,
but I don't want to "Orf." I just want to "Clang."

He thought the wharf was truly grand
as they visited every seafood stand.

He tried to Clang but could only wail
three little words, "Fish for Sale."

At Pier 39 they met a mime
and together they had a wonderful time.

Clyde thought he could help, without a doubt.
So he tried to Clang but nothing came out.

He swam with Sasha out to Seal Rocks
where swarms of Sea Gulls fly down in flocks.
As a group they swooped over Ocean Beach
while Clyde tried to "Clang" but could only go "Screech!"

On the Golden Gate Bridge that goes to Marin, Clyde heard the traffic's musical din.

To join with the foghorns down below he went "Blatt" and "Beep" and a deep "Eeeee-oh!"

To the sorrowful sound of the foghorn's wail he took a Ferry to Alcatraz Jail.

The island prison filled him with fear and Clyde just cried, "Get me out of here!"

On Fillmore Street he heard some jazz and came out with a sound that went "Razz-a-Matazz"

In Chinatown he
met a boy

who taught him to say
"Gung Hay Fat Choy."*

(At a Kosher Deli he just
said "Oy").

*Happy Chinese New Year!

Finding his
Clang would
really be neat
if he did it on
Lombard, the world's
crookedest street.

The curves were awesome,
the street was busy and all
he could say was "Boy am I dizzy!"

At the SF Zoo he searched some more when
the Lions let out a terrible ROAR.

The tiger cats woke and growled
for their chow.
But all Clyde could make
was a tiny "meow."

The monkeys thought it was only a trick
and a gang of Hyenas laughed themselves sick.

Sighed Clyde, "these sounds won't
get me far. I'm not a beast.
I'm a cable car."

The following day he paid a call
on the beautiful Davies Symphony Hall.

The musicians there were very nice
and quickly give him their advice.

The conductor said, "Clyde, if you follow me
you'll be a Cable Car Symphony."

So he opened his mouth and caused a fuss
with Beethoven, Brahms and "The Wheels on the Bus."

Clyde took a ride to old North Beach
to dine with a friend named Tony.

He laughed and sang, but still couldn't "Clang,"
he just called out "macaroni"

At Golden Gate Park, which is like none other, he heard some birds that tweet one another.

He tried to Clang but all he could do was cheep and warble and whistle and coo.

Soon he Came to the Merry Go Round
with wooden horses that made no sound.

But they all broke up with a "Ha. Ha. Ha."
when Clyde sounded off with an "Ooom-pah-pah."

He went to watch football and sat in the stands to hear the cheers of the loyal fans.

He hoped his "Clang" would at last come out but "Let's Go Niners" was all he could shout.

He then discovered, the very
next day, a world of miracles
right on the Bay:

The Exploratorium where
people learned how
our whole planet works
and he just went "Wow!"

He took in the Ballet and as you'd suppose, joined with the dancers up on his toes.

They whirled and swirled through a wonderful show but Clyde couldn't "Clang." He just bellowed "BRAVO!"

At Mission Dolores where goodness dwells, along with the sound of beautiful bells,

Clyde tried to Clang out his Cable Car song but could only go "Ding." And then he went "Dong."

Next came a truly miraculous thing. He heard the Bluebird of Happiness sing. Clyde opened his mouth about to shout, and what do you know, his Clang rang out!

"It's back!" he cried, "Let's give a cheer. At last my missing Clang is here!"

Now climbing the hills, up and down,
he could hear the sounds of this magical town.

With a "clickety-clack" and "Cling" and a "Clang,"
Clyde was the pride of the cable car gang.